ORION THE STAR

THE NIGHT BEFORE CHRISTMAS

BY JAMIE SKEIE

Orion the Star is one of the strongest superheroes in the world. Orion is always there, in every country in the world and in every universe. Orion is an entity powered by the stars and known as Orion's Belt.

This super-star parrot needs to save Christmas. Santa is down and out and Rudolph's nose isn't shining.

As Rudolph and Santa stand beside each other at the North Pole, they gaze into the stars in desperation and admiration.

They look at each other and then suddenly, as they look towards Orion's Belt at the stroke of midnight, they see a shooting star.

The star flew straight out of the ultraviolet night's sky like an arrow shooting from a bow.

This star shot through the sky right towards Santa and Rudolph. Suddenly, giant wings started to appear. It was not only a shooting star, but it was also Orion the Star!

Santa and Rudolph didn't know what to do. You'd think they had just seen Bigfoot!

Orion the Star is as big as a Sasquatch. Orion is fierce, fair, soft, and kind. Orion the Star is one of the most gentle mythical creatures ever known to man, spirit, and sanction of stars.

Orion landed smoothly and fast at the North Pole, right beside them. Rudolph's nose started sparkling red again. Santa didn't see because he was starring at Orion the Star.

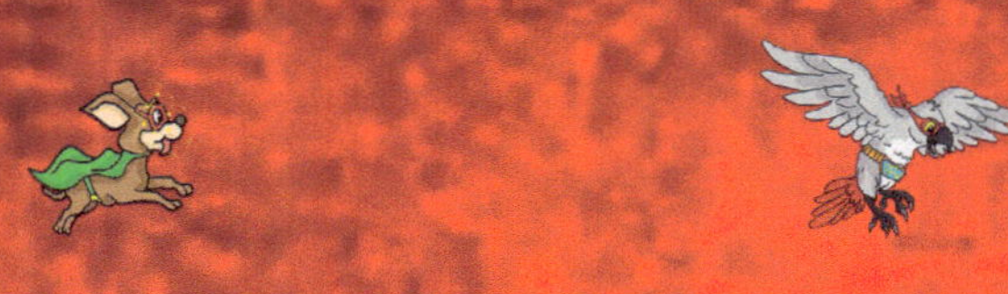

Santa said softly, "But, Orion..Rudolph's nose won't shine red, and the other reindeers won't fly."

Orion the Star replied, "It's because they need to have the faith the size of a birdseed. I know something that will get their attention."

Orion the Star whistled, and shouted and called them by name: "Now, Canis Major, and Canis Minor!"

As soon as the whistle was heard, the constellations beside Orion's Belt started to shine bright. As this mythical giant belted out their names, two dogs came barking, from the night's colorful sky.

Canis Major, tongue out like Jordan, tore down through the night's rising sky. This giant puppy dog had a magical red basketball that bounced against the clouds.

This dog dribbled down from the sky and suddenly went up for a slam dunk right next to a basketball hoop that suddenly appeared.

The basketball hoop was a gift from Santa. Santa had always heard about the stars and how they were real. He even believed his sleigh was powered and set on the navigation to deliver gifts on the night before Christmas, by the constellations powers.

Santa had heard the rumors of Orion the Star, Canis Major, Canis Minor, and the other constellations. In case these stars really were real; Santa and his special elves created the best gifts for these magical superstars.

Normally, Canis Major makes a sloppy landing, 'cause he can't dunk his basketball like Jordan, 'cause he has no hoop.

Canis Major sees the basketball hoop standing strong and hight beside the crew. Slobber comes off from both sides of the dog's mouth and a burst of happiness comes from within this superstar dog.

Canis Major strikes a pose as he flies through the air and dunks the ball like a dream.

Canis Major bounces to Santa Claus and can't resist jumping on the bearded man and slobbering as he replies, "You're a cool guy. Thank you, Santa! I've always wanted a basketball hoop!"

The crew all looked up into a smaller star flying towards them. This small star was flying in perfect formation. Santa looked to Orion the Star and winked. All at once, a library appeared beside the court, drifting on top of a gentle cloud.

Canis Major is a little dog, with a big personality. This superstar is brilliant and bright and always dreamed of a cloud library.

Never making an error in flight, this dog dropped its jaws, and dropped far from the sky, straight down until it landed on a little cloud. The cloud took the dog right to its dream library. The cloud library had everything.

The library even had every book from every universe. Some of the books were thousands of years old. Canis Minor thought he'd read all the books from every world and universe. He had a trillion years of reading ahead of him.

After a brief moment of delight, Canis Minor pounced towards Santa like a leopard. "Mr. Santa Claus, I would like to take a moment to thank you. You mean so much to everyone in the world. We all look up to you. You are the real star, Santa. You, Mrs. Claus, all the beautiful reindeer, and awesome elves. The world and the stars love all of you."

Before Canis Minor finished his prepared speech to Santa, a mound of Santa's elves all peeked out and started running out to surround the entourage.

In a New York second, the reindeer's stables started making scurry. A bright red light started shining. It was Dasher, Dancer, Prancer, Vixen, Comet, Cupid, Donner, Blixen, Blitzen, and Rudolph.

These reindeer flew straight out of the stables and dashed around the sky like hummingbirds in the springtime. These free spirits were flying around, happy again, for they knew Christmas was saved.

Orion the Star looked to Santa and replied, "Sometimes, it just takes a person to believe in milk and cookies."

Orion and Santa gave each other a big hug as everyone dashed around preparing for the night before Christmas, for all the mythical creatures in the Universe, were going to be there.

All the wonders of the world laughed, played, told stories, ate, and shared gifts with one another. They all got to open one present that Santa made come true. It was a beautiful day and a lovely night.

Orion the Star looked to Santa and replied, "Sometimes, it just takes a person to believe in milk and cookies."

Orion and Santa gave each other a big hug as everyone dashed around preparing for the night before Christmas, for all the mythical creatures in the Universe, were going to be there.

All the wonders of the world laughed, played, told stories, ate, and shared gifts with one another. They all got to open one present that Santa made come true. It was a beautiful day and a lovely night.

As quick as a star twinkles and shoots from the sky, Santa, Dasher, Dancer, Prancer, Vixen, Comet, Cupid, Donner, Blixen, Blitzen, Rudolph, Major, Minor, and Orion the Star dashed into the sky.

Santa and his new crew were on his sleigh. Together, they were going to bring love into the world the night before Christmas.

ORION THE STAR

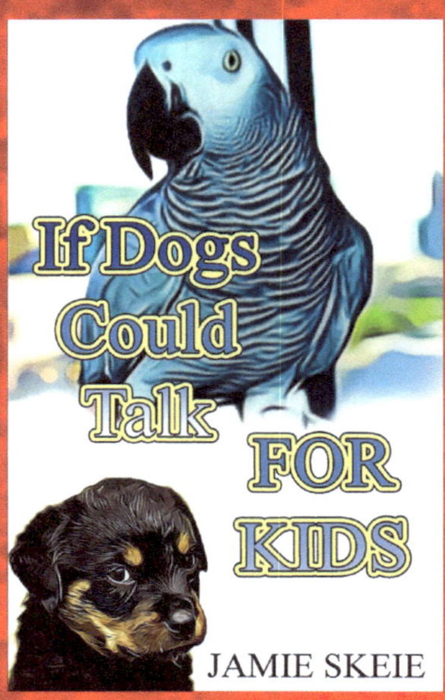

IF DOGS COULD TALK FOR KIDS and BIRD BRAINS are a colorful books, that showcase animal intelligence. An African Grey Congo parrot, Orion, was observed in her home for a year. All of her words were documented, and written down, word for word. You can study Orion's intelligence, and laugh at the things Orion says!

ABC
WORD
&
SENTENCE
BOOKS

ORION THE STAR is a children's book series for kids, dogs, parrots, cats, and even adults. Orion is a superstar parrot who flies from the stars to save any creature in distress. Orion's trusty sidekicks are two dogs named Canis Major and Canis Minor.

BOOK 1

BOOK 2

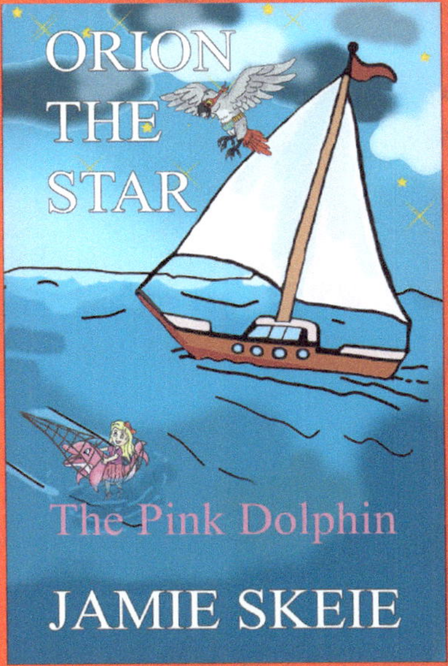

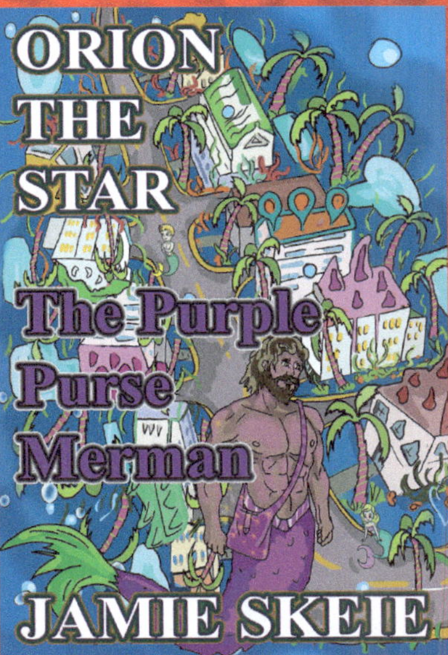

THE PINK DOLPHIN is a heartwarming dad and daughter sailing adventure. A beautiful girl dreams of mermaids, dolphins and heart-shaped pancakes. Awakening to the sweet aroma of her dad cooking pancakes, she feels happy and safe. After breakfast, they begin their sailing excursion. Along the way, the daughter spies a pink dolphin caught in a fishing net. The dolphin needs help, and this little girl is determined to save her. They have to endure a huge wave crashing into them as a caravan of sharks seize them without due process. As Dad fights to save himself from the sharks to save his daughter, Orion and the loyal dogs come to the rescue. This children's book, Orion the Star: The Pink Dolphin, showcases the never-ending love between a dad and his daughter.

THE PURPLE PURSE MERMAN features a story about a parallel universe. A father and son are going on a camping trip, right when a purple merman encounters a flying superstar parrot. This parrot is named, Orion the Star. Orion flies from the constellation, Orion's Belt. Orion has two trusty sidekicks, dogs named Canis Major, and Canis Minor. These universal superstars help reunite and help families, dogs, parrots and all the creatures in distress. The Purple Purse Merman feels very insecure being purple and having a purple purse that glitters and glistens. The story makes you realize, everyone has a little purple in them. That's what makes every creature different and special. Being purple is about embracing life and the creatures you love.

9 781672 381482